For Jason, my forever friend
~CF
For Anna, with all my love
~BC

Text Copyright © 2007 by Claire Freedman
Illustration Copyright © 2007 by Ben Cort
Published by arrangement with Simon & Schuster UK Ltd
1st Floor, 222 Gray's Inn Road, London, WC1X 8HB
A CBS Company

Dual language text copyright © 2011 Mantra Lingua
Audio copyright © 2011 Mantra Lingua
This edition 2011 All rights reserved
A CIP record for this book is available from the British Library
Mantra Lingua, Global House, 303 Ballards Lane, London, N12 8NP

www.mantralingua.com

Hear each page of this talking book narrated in many languages
with TalkingPEN! Then record your own versions.

Touch the arrow below with the TalkingPEN to start

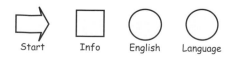

Start   Info   English   Language

外星人喜愛內褲
Aliens Love Underpants

Claire Freedman & Ben Cort

Traditional Chinese (Cantonese) translation by Sylvia Denham

Mantra Lingua

外星人喜愛內褲，
不論任何形狀和尺碼，
可是太空沒有內褲，
那真是一個很大的驚訝 …

Aliens love underpants,
Of every shape and size.
But there are no underpants in space,
So here's a big surprise...

當外星人飛到地球時，
他們並非為跟你會面才來到 …
他們只是想要你的內褲
– 這一點我肯定你從來不知道！

When aliens fly down to Earth, they don't come to meet YOU…
They simply want your underpants - I'll bet you never knew!

一旦探測到有內褲在曬衣繩上隨風飄揚，
太空船的雷達便立時嘟嘟發響閃閃發亮。

Their spaceship's radar bleeps and blinks the moment that it sees
A washing line of underpants all flapping in the breeze.

即使未被邀請，他們會在你的後園降落著陸，
「哦，內褲呀！」他們高興地唱歌跳舞慶祝。

They land in your back garden, though they haven't been invited.
"Oooooh, UNDERPANTS!" they chant, and dance around, delighted.

他們喜歡紅色的、綠色的，還有橘橙色，
但最喜歡的還是婆婆那斑點燈籠褲的款式。

They like them red, they like them green, or orange like satsumas.
But best of all they love the sight of Granny's spotted bloomers.

媽媽的粉紅色花邊內褲是最適宜躲藏的地方，
而公公的羊毛長內褲卻是最超極的滑坡。

Mum's pink frilly knickers are a perfect place to hide
And Grandpa's woolly longjohns make a super-whizzy slide.

In daring competitions, held up by just one peg,
They count how many aliens can squeeze inside each leg.

他們刺激地擠進那靠一隻
衣夾揪著的長內褲裡，
然後點算有多少外星人能
往每一邊褲管擠進去。

他們將內褲穿在腳上和頭上，還有其他可笑的地方，
他們把內褲懸掛在太空船上，更穿著內褲倒立賽跑！

They wear pants on their feet and heads and other silly places.
They fly pants from their spaceships and hold Upside-Down-Pant Races!

當他們在空中團團轉時，
那簡直是奇裝異服，
外星人更把褲腰的橡皮圈
玩弄得不亦樂乎！

As they go zinging through the air,
it really is pants-tastic.
What fun the aliens can have
with pingy pants elastic!

這並不是鄰家頑皮的狗兒或是街坊的玩意，
內褲不見了，都要怪外星人所作的事！

It's not your neighbour's naughty dog, or next-door's funny game.
When underpants go missing, the ALIENS are to blame!

But quick! Mum's coming out to fetch the washing in at last.
Wheee! Off the aliens all zoom, they're used to leaving fast...

但是快啊！快啊！
媽媽終於出來收取衣服了，
嘻嘻！外星人全部立時飛走，
他們都習慣快速地溜掉 …

在你穿上你剛剛洗得乾淨清潔的內褲前，
記得檢查一下，萬一還有外星人躲在裡面看不見！

So when you put your pants on, freshly washed and nice and clean,
Just check in case an alien still lurks inside, unseen!